This TWO HOOTS book

belongs to

FOR SARAH AND SARAH

x x

First published 2018 by Two Hoots
This edition published 2019 by Two Hoots
an imprint of Pan Macmillan
20 New Wharf Road, London N1 9RR
Associated companies throughout the world
www.panmacmillan.com
ISBN 978-1-5098-3484-6

1 3 5 7 9 8 6 4 2
A CIP catalogue record for this book is available from the British Library.
Printed in China
The illustrations in this book were created using lino print and collage.

www.twohootsbooks.com

THE STEVES

MORAG HOOD

TWO HOOTS

Hello! I'm Steve.

I'M Steve.

But I was
here first.

**BY ONE
PAGE!**

I am Steve.
You can be
Steve the
Second.

I am Steve
the First,

and I'll prove it.

When's your birthday?

Sixth of March . . .

AH HA! I'm older
than you. I am Steve!
I am the greatest.

I'm wiser.

I'm taller.

How many fish can you catch?

More than you.
I am the Champion
of Steves.
The Stevest
Steve.

I am the fastest. The strongest. The best.
The one and only. I AM STEVE.

You've got
weird feet.

WEIRD
FEET
STEVE!

Well, you
smell.

SMELLS
OF
POO
STEVE.

I don't smell
of poo.

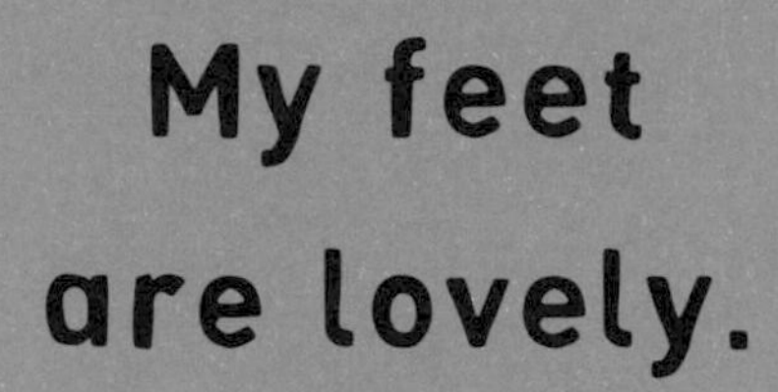

My feet
are lovely.

Sorry, Steve.

Sorry, Steve.

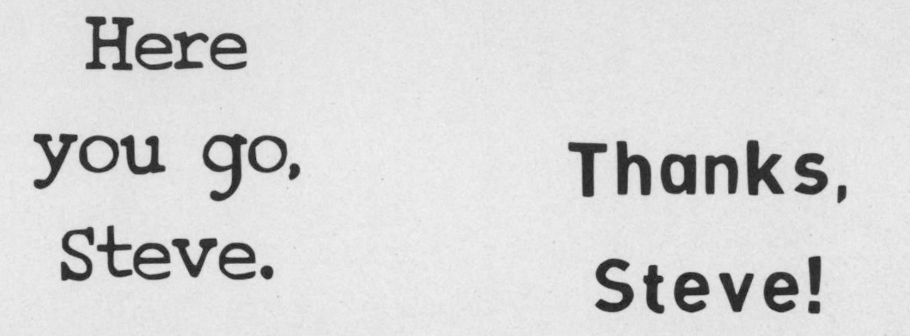
Here you go, Steve.
Thanks, Steve!

Hello!

I'm Steve.

- A puffin weighs the same as a can of cola
- Baby puffins are called pufflings
- Puffins live in a hole in the ground called a burrow
- When puffins are angry they stomp their feet

They're my facts too!